Story Adaptations by Etta Wilson
Illustrations by Bob Singer
Art Direction by Linda Karl

MALLARD PRESS
An Imprint of BDD Promotional Book Company, Inc.
666 Fifth Avenue
New York, N.Y. 10103

"Mallard Press and its accompanying design and logo
are trademarks of BDD Promotional Book Company, Inc."

Story Adaptations by March Media, Inc.
Illustrations by Singer/Bandy Group
Produced by Hamilton Projects, Inc.

ISBN 0-792-45154-6

Printed in the United States

MALLARD
PRESS

THE BIG BREAK

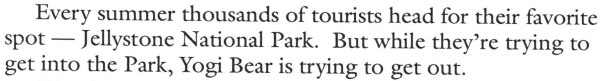

Every summer thousands of tourists head for their favorite spot — Jellystone National Park. But while they're trying to get into the Park, Yogi Bear is trying to get out.

"I've had it," Yogi said to his little friend Boo Boo. "Every day it's the same old thing — tourists driving by saying 'look at the bears,' 'look at the bears.' I'm leaving!"

"How are you going to get past the ranger, Yogi?"

"I'll use strategy, Boo. Watch this," said Yogi.

3

First Yogi tried to sneak past the ranger's window on the back of a car. Then Yogi dressed up to look like someone leaving the Park in a trailer. He even tried looking like a dead bear being taken out by a hunter.

But the ranger caught on to each of Yogi's tricks.

Boo Boo thought it was time for Yogi to give up.
"No," said Yogi, "I'm smarter than the average bear!"
His next plan called for using a pole to go over the wall.
He might have made it except for a gopher hole.

Then he tried going under the wall, but his map was not quite right and Yogi made a surprise visit inside the ranger's station.

When Yogi found a tall tree near the park wall, he thought up a smart new plan. He strapped on a parachute, tied himself to the tree, and asked Boo Boo to spring him over the wall.

"Pull the rope, Boo Boo, and I'm out of here!"

"Don't forget to write, Yogi," called Boo Boo.

It worked! Yogi was out of the Park, but not for long!
His parachute brought him down on a big truck headed right
into the gate.

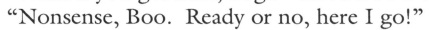

Yogi was desperate. He had only one plan left. He set up a hollow log like a cannon aimed over the wall, covered his head with a helmet, and crawled into the log. Then he called down to Boo Boo to light the fuse at the bottom.

"What if you get hurt, Yogi?" asked Boo Boo.

"Nonsense, Boo. Ready or no, here I go!"

Just as Boo Boo lit the fuse, Ranger Smith came by and asked where Yogi was. Before Boo Boo could think of an excuse for Yogi, the ranger told him it was the first day of hunting season. Yogi was very lucky to be *inside* the Park.

The log exploded! Yogi was outside the Park at last!
But so were the hunters. In just a few minutes Yogi was
running back to the park gate.
"Hey, open up," he yelled. "It's me. I belong in there. I
love the Park!"

THE ICE BOX RAIDER

Yogi Bear is always looking for a free meal, and his favorite food is in Ranger Smith's refrigerator.

Yogi and his little buddy Boo Boo were watching the ranger's station, hoping for a chance to slip in for goodies.

"My plans are laid for an ice box raid," Yogi said, "if those rangers ever come out of there."

But Ranger Smith was tired of Yogi's raids. He and Ranger Jones were laying a trap in the refrigerator.
"We'll catch him barehanded — Yogi Bear-handed, that is," Ranger Smith laughed.

15

As soon as the rangers left, Yogi headed for the station and the refrigerator.

"The ice box raider strikes again!" he said to Boo Boo. But when he opened the door, he didn't find goodies!

Yogi was very mad that he got caught. And right outside the door he had to walk past the laughing rangers.

"There's guilt written all over you, Yogi. In wet paint!" said Ranger Smith.

But Yogi Bear was determined to prove that he was smarter than the average bear. For a week he stayed busy in his cave, sewing on a fur rug from the Jellystone Park Inn. Boo Boo wanted to know what Yogi was making.

"I've made me a double to cause some trouble, Hey, Hey, Hey! This week I get even with the ranger!"

Yogi and Boo Boo carried the dummy bear through the woods and up the cliff to Lover's Leap. They set up the dummy on the edge, tied one end of a ball of string around the dummy, and threw the ball over the cliff. Then they hurried down so Yogi could pull the string to make the dummy move back and forth, back and forth.

The tourists were sure a bear was about to jump over the cliff, and called the ranger from the nearest phone.

Before Ranger Smith could get to the bottom of the cliff, Yogi had thrown the dummy in the bushes and taken its place. He looked almost dead when the ranger came running up.

"This is all my fault," said Ranger Smith. "I shouldn't have put that paint in the refrigerator. Yogi, speak to me! Say you forgive me."

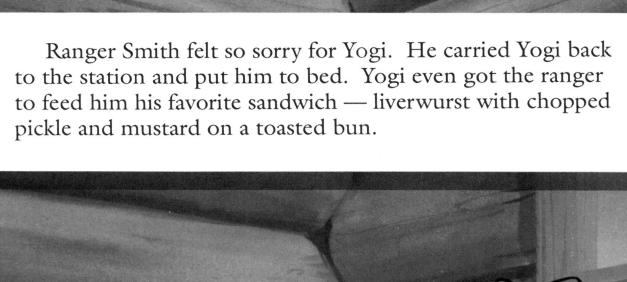

Ranger Smith felt so sorry for Yogi. He carried Yogi back to the station and put him to bed. Yogi even got the ranger to feed him his favorite sandwich — liverwurst with chopped pickle and mustard on a toasted bun.

21

Outside the station, Boo Boo saw Ranger Jones coming from the woods with the dummy bear. Yogi's little buddy knew there was trouble ahead for Yogi.

'Sir," called Ranger Jones, "I think I've found the bear rug that is missing from the Inn."

It didn't take Ranger Smith long to figure out Yogi's trick. "I'll bet you found that stuffed rug below Lover's Leap," he said. "Now I'm going in to take care of Yogi!"

Yogi heard enough through the front door to know that it was time for him to travel — out the back door. He was gone when the rangers came in. They decided to chase him in their jeep.

"It won't start!" said Ranger Smith.

"Let's check it. It may be something simple," Ranger Jones suggested.

When Ranger Smith lifted the front of the jeep, Yogi had a surprise waiting for him! It was Yogi's turn to laugh. "That painter's brush sure stopped their rush. Hey, Hey, Hey!"

SPY GUY

The ranger station at Jellystone Park has been the scene of much activity all night. Ranger Smith has installed a TV camera and microphone at every trouble spot in the Park.

"Now I can keep an eye on that trouble-making bear. Yogi can't make a move without my seeing him on the TV," the Ranger said to himself. "I'll tune in and have some fun."

Yogi and Boo Boo had headed for the picnic area early that morning. Yogi was hungry as usual. "Look, little bear buddy, it's a pic-a-nic basket! And roast chicken."

As Yogi took his first bite, he heard a voice from a hidden speaker. "Yogi Bear, this is the voice of your conscience."

Yogi thought it was Boo Boo, but it wasn't.

"Yogi! You stole that roast chicken from a picnic basket," the voice said. "Put it back and leave the area at once!"

Yogi decided he and Boo Boo should visit the inn kitchen next. He was determined to find goodies, and he didn't know that Ranger Smith was watching them every place they went.

"Stand back, Boo, while I check the ice box," said Yogi. "The ranger doesn't know we're here."

Just then Yogi heard the voice again. "Get your paw off that door, Yogi! You know you're not supposed to be in the kitchen."

Yogi and Boo Boo headed for the tourist cabins next. Yogi was still hungry.

"What about your conscience, Yogi?" Boo Boo asked.

"I'm smarter than my conscience, Boo Boo, buddy."

"Hold it, Yogi!" It was the voice again. "You know it's against the rules to bother the tourists!"

The only place to look for food was in the woods, and Yogi had to have more to eat than that. He went to find the ranger and tell him that the Park was haunted!

But as Yogi and Boo Boo arrived at the station, they heard Ranger Smith laughing and talking about the trick he had played on Yogi.

"The TV setup is working swell! I can see every move Yogi makes, and he thinks I'm the voice of his conscience," the ranger was saying.

Yogi caught on right away. "Let's go, Boo Boo! There's work to do-do-do!"

First Yogi and Boo Boo went to the ranger's station and removed some tubes from the TV.

"Let's head for the pic-a-nic area, Boo. Hey, hey, hey!"

A short while later, Ranger Smith got a telephone call.

"What! Every picnic basket in the Park has disappeared. The tourists are rioting? Oh, no! Yogi Bear has struck back! I'll be right there."

Yogi and Boo Boo returned to the station and replaced the TV tubes. Then they could see the ranger in front of the angry tourists. The ranger was having trouble, and Yogi knew he had a chance to get even. After all, he was smarter than the average bear.

"Attention, Mr. Ranger, Sir. If you want those pic-a-nic baskets back, how about making a deal?" Yogi said into the microphone.

The next morning Ranger Smith came to Yogi's cave with a king-size picnic basket loaded with goodies and roast chicken.

"Here you are, Yogi. You'll get one every morning for two weeks!" the ranger said.

"Gee, Yogi, this is like breakfast in bed," said Boo Boo.

"It's even better, Boo, my buddy. It's in a pic-a-nic basket!"

SLUMBER PARTY SMARTY

When Mother Nature covers Jellystone Park with a blanket of snow, it's time for Yogi Bear to hit the hay for his long winter's nap. He had set the alarm clock for spring.

Yogi was just about to crawl into bed when he heard someone call.

"Mister Bear!"

Yakky Doodle was on his doorstep.

"Can I stay here with you, can I?" the little duck asked.
"Aren't you ducks supposed to fly south for the winter?
And us bears have to sleep all winter. I can't have you
knocking around my cave," said Yogi.
Yakky Doodle begged and begged, but Yogi refused.
"No can do! Shoo!"

The little biddy duck walked away in the snow.
"Ah-Choo! It's cold outside. Ah-Choo! Ah-Choo!"
Yogi's heart melted. "Come on back. you can stay, but
remember — one peep and out you go."

Yogi soon discovered that it was not easy to share his bed with a duck. The little duck liked a lot of room!

Yogi decided to put the little duck to sleep in a different bed, but it wasn't far enough away when Yakky Doodle started to snore.

Next Yogi put the little duck to sleep on the mantle over the fire. Everything was dark when Yakky Doodle woke up and saw something walking in the dark. He wanted to protect his new friend Yogi.

"I caught a bear! I caught a — Uh Oh!"
"I know," said Yogi, "I know!"

In a little while the cave began to feel cold. Yakky Doodle wanted to build a fire, but he needed more wood. "Okay, okay," said Yogi, "but chop your own wood and keep it quiet!"

Yakky Doodle chopped very fast — and very loud. Yogi went out to tell him to quit the chopping, but it was too late! The tree was coming down!

Being smarter than the average bear, Yogi decided there was only one way to get some sleep.

"Hey, Mister Bear, you going somewhere?" asked Yakky.

"If you're going to say *here*, I'm going *there* — south, that is! I've gotta get my winter's nap!" said Yogi.

"Hey! Hey! Hey!"